Mighty Machines
Trains

by Matt Doeden

Consulting Editor: Gail Saunders-Smith, PhD

Consultant: Bob R. Tucker
General Manager of Train Handling (Retired)
Railway Operating Officers Association

Capstone
press

Mankato, Minnesota

Pebble Plus is published by Capstone Press,
151 Good Counsel Drive, P.O. Box 669, Mankato, Minnesota 56002.
www.capstonepress.com

1 2 3 4 5 6 11 12 10 09 08 07

Library of Congress Cataloging-in-Publication Data
Doeden, Matt.
  Trains / by Matt Doeden.
    p. cm.—(Pebble Plus. Mighty machines)
  Includes bibliographical references and index.
  ISBN-13: 978-0-7368-6722-1 (hardcover)
  ISBN-10: 0-7368-6722-8 (hardcover)
  1. Railroads—Trains—Juvenile literature. I. Title. II. Series.
TF148.D64 2007
625.1—dc22   2006014718

Summary: Simple text and photographs describe trains, their parts, and what they do.

Editorial Credits

Mari Schuh, editor; Molly Nei, set designer; Patrick D. Dentinger, book designer; Jo Miller, photo researcher/
    photo editor

Photo Credits

Corbis/Morton Beebe, cover; Premium Stock, 17; Richard T. Nowitz, 14–15
David R. Frazier Photolibrary Inc., 4–5
The Image Finders, 8–9, Howard Ande, 10–11, 19
Lynn M. Stone, 6–7
PhotoEdit Inc./Jeff Greenberg, 12–13
Shutterstock/Ryan Parent, 1; Wade H. Massie, 20–21

Note to Parents and Teachers

The Mighty Machines set supports national social studies standards related to science, technology, and society. This book describes and illustrates trains. The images support early readers in understanding the text. The repetition of words and phrases helps early readers learn new words. This book also introduces early readers to subject-specific vocabulary words, which are defined in the Glossary section. Early readers may need assistance to read some words and to use the Table of Contents, Glossary, Read More, Internet Sites, and Index sections of the book.

Table of Contents

Trains

A train is a long line
of railroad cars
hooked together.
Trains move on tracks.

Parts of Trains

Trains have wheels
that fit over railroad tracks.
Railroad tracks
are long steel rails.

CSS 30334

CSS
3033

7

Locomotives pull trains.

The train's engine

sits inside the locomotive.

Railroad cars make up
the longest part of a train.
Freight cars carry goods.
Passenger cars carry people.

Choo! Choo!

Trains have loud whistles.

Whistles warn people

that a train is coming.

Kinds of Trains

Commuter trains carry people
on short trips.
Subway trains
run under city streets.

Passenger trains carry people

for thousands of miles.

People can eat and sleep

on these trains.

Freight trains carry coal,
grain, and other goods
across the country.

Mighty Machines

Trains roll through tunnels
and under bridges.
Trains are mighty machines.

Glossary

freight train—a train that carries goods or cargo; some freight trains are more than a mile long.

goods—items that people buy and use; freight trains carry goods such as car parts, toys, and food.

locomotive—the railroad car that holds the engine to pull the train

subway train—a kind of train that runs under the ground

track—a set of rails for trains to run on

tunnel—a passage made under the ground or through a mountain for use by trains and cars

whistle—an object that makes a high, loud sound; cars and trucks should not cross railroad tracks when a train is blowing its whistle.

Read More

Riggs, Kate. *Trains.* My First Look at Vehicles. Mankato, Minn.: Creative Education, 2007.

Schaefer, Lola M. *Trains.* Wheels, Wings, and Water. Chicago: Heinemann, 2003.

Tieck, Sarah. *Trains.* Mighty Movers. Edina, Minn.: Abdo, 2005.

Internet Sites

FactHound offers a safe, fun way to find Internet sites related to this book. All of the sites on FactHound have been researched by our staff.

Here's how:

1. Visit *www.facthound.com*

2. Choose your grade level.

3. Type in this book ID **0736867228** for age-appropriate sites. You may also browse subjects by clicking on letters, or by clicking on pictures and words.

4. Click on the **Fetch It** button.

FactHound will fetch the best sites for you!

Index

Word Count: 122
Grade: 1
Early-Intervention Level: 13